QUICKLY
THE MAGIC SPATULA

To Scott...

Award Winning Team:

Jeryl Abelmann & Miriam Kronish

Illustrated by **Chason Matthams**

May Quickly spark treasured family Memories...

Jeryl Abelmann

Summary: A family story is remembered when an antique is discovered in the attic.

Text copyright © 2008 by Jeryl Abelmann and Miriam Kronish
First Edition copyright © 2009
Second Edition copyright © 2010
Third Edition copyright © 2011

Illustrations copyright © 2008 by Chason Matthams

Design by Daniel J. Seward.

The Dancing Mommy image is a registered trademark belonging to Jeryl Abelmann.

Visit us on the web!
www.QuicklyTheMagicSpatula.com | www.QuicklysMagicalPancakeAdventure.com

Printed in China

ISBN 978-0-9971084-0-8 Paperback
ISBN 978-0-9971084-1-5 Hardcover
ISBN 978-0-9971084-4-6 ebook

Published by:
Dancing Mommy Press
P.O. Box 321
Pebble Beach, CA 93953
www.DancingMommyPress.com

Dedicated to children everywhere

who have stories in their hearts just waiting to be told

To Nancy

who started us on our journey

To Charlotte, Holden, Danielle, and Rochelle

whose journeys have just begun …

The kitchen is a special place —
the heart of the home — the hearth,
where hunger is heartily handled,
where memories are made, and
where this story originates.

Of all of our senses,
the olfactory is the most memorable.
Just an aroma quickly sensed can trigger
whole scenes from childhood.
And this is where we want to carry you —
back to when you were little.

Come with us to Mommy's kitchen —
and after your visit, back to your own.

My brother Jeff and I used to love to play in our attic at the top of the stairs. Fun beckoned as we watched the warm sun shine through the attic window. We loved watching the shadows as they stretched across the floor.

The sun warmed us as we played hide and seek among the boxes, sang songs, and laughed at silly riddles. We loved to read poetry to each other, color pictures, play board games on the floor, and do our homework on the cozy old comfortable sofa.

The years went by fast, as they do, and now Jeff and I were all grown up. There we sat, back in our old attic, searching through dusty boxes that were carefully stored away years ago. The boxes were filled with treasures just waiting to be discovered.

The shadows stretched across the attic floor as the sun continued to shine through the window. Jeff and I were having fun talking about the past as we sifted through the dusty boxes.

Suddenly, we came upon a box that was filled with Mommy's old kitchen utensils.

As we looked through the box, we both spied something special. My brother and I smiled and shouted at the same time: "Quickly! It's Quickly!"

What we found was an old silver spatula with a few flecks of green paint on its wooden handle. Although worn by time and touched by age, here was Quickly in my brother's hands again after so many years.

It wasn't sparkly any more, it wasn't green any more, and it was very crooked. When we were little, it had been sparkly and green and straight as could be.

Memories of Quickly raced through our minds … and memories of Mommy's kitchen … the sunlight coming through the window … the clicking of Mommy's high heels as she bustled around the kitchen … the smell of those sizzling hot pancakes.

We were transported to another time, many years ago, before Quickly had become a household name. Our memories found us in our childhood home and we were little once again.

By the time we woke up on Sundays, Mommy had already been up for hours and was always doing the same thing — making our favorite pancakes.

Somehow, no one could get up earlier than Mommy. She was dressed for the occasion with her apron tied neatly around her waist. Even on those early Sunday mornings, Mommy had on her high heels. Mommy said it was because she liked to feel tall.

Sunday after Sunday, pancake after pancake, we loved watching Mommy making her pancakes — and we loved eating them, too.

First, Mommy would make a large pot of coffee for the grownups. Then she assembled all the ingredients for the pancakes. She measured everything very carefully and mixed it in the bowl.

Now it was cooking time. Mommy melted the butter on the griddle. She leaned her shiny silver spatula up against the griddle so that it would be ready to flip the pancakes.

It was very important for Mommy to have that spatula right there to make sure that the pancakes never burned.

In her high heels, with the green wooden handle of her sparkly spatula held firmly in her hand, Mommy was prepared.

And then one Sunday morning something happened. Mommy had forgotten to lean her shiny silver spatula up against the griddle.

Jeff and I were waiting. Mommy had started the pancakes. The batter was sizzling when she suddenly called to my brother …

"Jeffrey! Jeffrey! Please get me the spatula … quickly!"

He grabbed the spatula and ran across the kitchen. As he ran, he yelled, "Here Mommy, here's Quickly!" Four-year-old Jeff thought that "Quickly" was the spatula's name!

From that Sunday morning on, the spatula was
no longer just a spatula; this sparkly green and
silver tool had a name — Quickly!

"Yesssss!" thought Quickly. "I'm no longer
just a spatula — I have my own name!
I can make magic, I know I can!"

Quickly knew that there would be smiling faces in
our kitchen, anticipating what was coming.

From then on, every time Mommy picked Quickly up to make our Sunday pancakes, something extraordinary happened. Those pancakes — they seemed to taste more delicious than ever. The aroma wafting from the griddle, the sight of the pancakes, the texture of the batter — Quickly's magic spell made the batter taste better!

Everyone who ate them said that they had never tasted more wonderful pancakes. And even though other people borrowed the recipe and tried to make pancakes in their own kitchens, they NEVER tasted like Mommy's. Never!

And Quickly was the secret!

Many years passed. Mommy became a Grandma. Mommy's grandchildren loved her dearly and gave her a special name, too. They called her Grandma Darling.

As Grandma Darling grew older, so did Quickly. Quickly's luster had dimmed, and its green paint had started to peel, but it still did its job remarkably.

With Quickly close at hand, Grandma Darling continued to make her delicious Sunday morning pancakes for her grandchildren and everyone else who flocked to her door.

The years went by and Grandma Darling had a very full and happy life. She was adored by her children and grandchildren, respected and admired by all her friends, and at the age of eighty-six she died.

And Quickly was forgotten. Until this moment!

The sun was setting through the attic window and the shadows stretched across the attic just as they did when we were little. The box of kitchen utensils was on the floor and Quickly was in Jeff's hands.

Jeff clutched Quickly. I caught his smile, and I also saw tears of remembrance in his eyes. He was remembering Mommy and that day when he was a little boy — a little boy who made us all smile by giving Quickly its magical name.

And now — here he was so many years later, once again holding Quickly.

In finding Quickly we found more than a spatula —
we recovered such special memories. Memories that
brought a smile to our lips and a tug at our hearts as
we remembered Mommy.

Jeff and I left the attic holding hands. And once again,
Jeff held onto Quickly, too, as he did so many years before.

We turned to each other and we both had the same
thought at the same time! Pancakes! We flew into the
kitchen to make a batch — and you know what?

They tasted extra specially good — now that
Quickly was there to help us.

Quickly is not in a kitchen drawer anymore. We put Quickly into a frame ... and today our dear little magical Quickly has a place of honor in our kitchen.

Our treasured spatula hangs on the wall with a sparkly silver sign that proudly reads "Quickly"!

My brother and I rediscovered magic in the attic that sunny day. A family story had returned!

Our Quickly story — a childhood memory — one that will live in our hearts forever.

And now you, dear reader — do you have a story about your family that you'd like to tell, or perhaps write down so that it can be saved and savored throughout the years? We'd love to hear it!

Please write your story to us at www.QuicklyTheMagicSpatula.com.

In anticipation,
Jeryl and Miriam

The following pages are for your story.

If you would like to share your story
please write to us.

www.QuicklyTheMagicSpatula.com

QUICKLY'S GLOSSARY

Do you have any questions for Quickly?
"Yes, I want to know what these words mean."
Here are Quickly's answers to your questions:

Anticipating: looking forward to

Aroma: mouth-watering smell

Batch: portion

Batter: all the makings mixed together

Beckoned: signaled to come forward

Bustled: moved about excitedly

Dimmed: lost its shine and color

Extraordinary: very special

Flocked: came in large groups

Griddle: a heavy flat iron frying pan

Honor: have deep respect for

Ingredients: everything that goes into the makings

Luster: shine

Magic: a quality that makes something seem removed from everyday life, especially in a way that gives delight

Olfactory: relating to sense of smell

Remarkably: worthy of being noticed

Remembrance: fixed in one's memory

Respected: very well thought of by others

Savored: loved the taste of

Sizzling: very hot

Spatula: a flat-bottomed cooking tool with holes

Texture: the feel and appearance of a substance

Transported: carried away to another place

Utensils: kitchen tools

Wafting: rising up of aroma from cooked food

Chef Quickly

Gold Medal Winner | *Quickly: The Magic Spatula*

Mommy's Silver Dollar Pancakes

Ingredients:

1 cup sour cream
1 cup cottage cheese
1 tablespoon maple syrup
½ teaspoon pure vanilla extract
4 large eggs, separated
1 tablespoon sugar
¾ cup flour
unsalted butter, for greasing the griddle

Preparation:

Combine sour cream, cottage cheese, maple syrup, vanilla extract, and egg yolks.

Beat thoroughly.

Slowly add flour to batter and continue to stir.

Add sugar to egg whites and beat until stiff. Fold into batter.

Lightly butter a griddle.

Ladle about 3 tablespoons of the batter for each silver dollar pancake.

Cook until the bottom side is nicely browned.

Turn pancake over and cook on the other side until browned.

Continue ladling the batter and cooking the pancakes until all the batter is used. Stir the batter from the bottom as the bottom is used to maintain the consistency.

If desired, add fruit to the batter, such as blueberries, strawberries, raspberries, banana slices, or a combination of fruit.

Serve them "quickly" with warmed maple syrup!

Serves 4 – 6

The Authors

Jeryl Abelmann is a retired elementary school teacher. She is the recipient of Teacher of the Year for the San Ramon Valley Unified School District in California. A member of The Carmel Bach Festival Board of Directors, the California Writers Club, and the Screen Actors Guild, she loves the movies, theater, writing, and traveling. She has two sons and four adorable grandchildren. She and her husband live in Northern California.

Miriam Kronish teaches at Cambridge College in Massachusetts. Over the past decades she has taught at Lesley University in the Creative Arts in Learning Master's Degree Program. She is a retired principal from the Needham (MA) Public Schools. Her interests are music, educational pursuits, cooking, theater, reading, and especially writing. She is a National Distinguished Principal and an Honored Principal in the State of Massachusetts. She is a Past President of the Needham Rotary Club. She lives in Massachusetts with her husband.

The Illustrator

Chason Matthams is the 2011 "Children's Books Winner" for his illustrations for *Quickly: The Magic Spatula* from the Hollywood Book Festival. He is a graduate of the Fine Arts Department of New York University. His artistic works include illustration, painting, and portraiture. He received his MFA in studio art from NYU where he continues to teach painting as an adjunct professor. He lives in New York City and has shown his artwork in galleries from New York to San Francisco.

The Authors' book *Quickly: The Magic Spatula* is the 2011 "Children's Books Winner" of the Hollywood Book Festival. *Quickly: The Magic Spatula* was named the Gold Medal Winner of the Moonbeam Children's Book Award from the Independent Publishing Industry. This award honors the best children's books that show dedication to children's literacy and inspired writing, illustrating, and publishing.

The Bay Area Independent Publishers Association named *Quickly: The Magic Spatula* **Best Children's Picture Book.**